Pooks and Boots

Teach about David and Goliath

Julie K. Wood

Illustrated by Simon Goodway

ISBN 978-1-63814-407-6 (Paperback)
ISBN 978-1-63814-408-3 (Digital)

Covenant Books, Inc.
11661 Hwy 707
Murrells Inlet, SC 29576
www.covenantbooks.com

Then said David to the Philistine, Thou comest to me with a sword, and with a spear, and with a shield: but I come to thee in the name of the Lord of hosts, the God of the armies of Israel, whom thou hast defied.

—1 Samuel 17:45 (KJV)

ichael dropped his backpack in the school hallway when he saw the poster for the Space Academy Science Competition! His eyes opened wide, reading the details as fast as he could. He was imagining calculations and formulas flashing all around in his mind. He knew the science project he won last year would help him find a creative solution for this competition. He put a finger on his chin and smiled confidently, as an imaginative vision came to mind on how to create a rocket invention that would improve spaceships for the astronauts! He could already see the rocket launching with his winning idea.

Quickly picking up his backpack, he grabbed a copy of the flyer and ran down the hall to see his teacher.

"Are you okay, Michael?" his teacher asked with confusion.

"The competition," Michael said, breathing heavy and waving the flyer in the air, "the competition, I want to enter the competition!"

"Oh, yes, the Space Academy Science Competition. Catch your breath, Michael. I love your excitement and confidence for this big event, but you are too young, and the older students have more experience," his teacher said with a regretful voice.

Michael frowned as he looked down. He crumpled up the flyer and put it in his pocket and began to walk home.

"I can't give up!" Michael thought to himself. He looked up at the sky and imagined rockets flying into space. Suddenly, a new thought entered his mind, "Wait! I know who can help. Pooks and Boots! They taught me how all things are possible with God!"

Michael knew they would be at the park and ran as fast as he could to find them!

Pooks and Boots were surprised as they saw Michael quickly approaching, waving a flyer in the air.

"I don't know for sure, but something tells me Michael has something important to say," Boots said to Pooks with a mouth full of kitty treats.

Pooks slowly closed the Bible she was reading with Kristy. "I think you are right, Boots. I have never seen Michael run. Ever."

"You have to help, you have to help," Michael said, catching his breath while waving the crumpled-up flyer in his little hand, "I want to enter the competition!"

Pooks calmly responded, "Slow down, slow down, it is going to be okay. Take a deep breath and tell me what you are talking about."

"My teacher said I can't enter the Space Academy Science Competition because I am too young and do not have enough experience." Michael handed Pooks the flyer and put his hands on his knees so he could catch his breath.

Handing Boots another kitty treat, Kristy gave Michael a hug. "I understand how you feel. I think I am too little to play basketball, but my coach wants me play."

Pooks held her Bible close to her chest. "We must all trust in God." She thought for a moment, "I think you both can get your answers from the story of David and Goliath."

Jumping up and down in the park, acting like she was swinging a sling around in the air, Boots shouted, "Yes, yes, David and Goliath is exactly the right story!"

"Settle down, Boots," Pooks said lovingly. "Let me share the story from the beginning so they understand how to trust in God with their situations."

Pooks calmly pointed at the blanket on the grass and said, "Let us all relax and sit down as I read from the Bible." She slowly turned the pages to the story of David and Goliath.

Michael and Kristy were eager to hear the story. Boots stuffed another kitty treat in her mouth and swallowed it whole without even chewing.

Pooks began. "It started with King Saul and his men of Israel in a battle against the Philistines. The Philistines stood on one side of the mountain, and the Israelites stood on the other side. The Philistines had a champion named Goliath, a nine-foot giant!"

Kristy's eyes grew large with amazement, "Goliath was nine feet tall? That's almost as high as a basketball hoop!"

Boots interrupted with excitement, "That's right, that's right, Goliath was really tall and had lots of heavy armor!" She jumped up and started swinging her paws around like she was in an imaginary battle with Goliath!

"Yes, Boots is correct," Pooks reached out with her paw to help Boots sit back down. "Goliath had a very heavy brass helmet, spear, and shield. He challenged the Israelites and yelled, 'Choose your best soldier to fight me. If he wins, we will become your servants, but if I win, you will become our servants.'"

Boots jumped up and down again, while chewing on another kitty treat, "Big old giant didn't know about David!"

"We have not gotten to David yet!" Pooks fussed at Boots as she continued to read. "So where was I… hmmm…oh, yes. There was a king by the name of King Saul. The king and all Israel heard Goliath's challenge, but they were afraid."

Pooks paused and held the Bible in the air. "Now here is where it gets really good!"

Looking to ensure everyone was listening closely, Pooks reopened her Bible and continued. "Now there was a father named Jesse. He had eight sons, and the youngest and smallest of them was David."

"Now we're talking! Here comes David! He was the youngest and the smallest of the sons!" Boots said with a full mouth. "That's right, that's right, the youngest and the smallest, but he's going to take down that giant!"

"Yes, Boots, that's right," Pooks continued despite the interruption. "But you're getting ahead of the story. David was the youngest and the smallest of Jesse's sons. In fact, the three oldest sons were in King Saul's army. However, David was a shepherd and was still home with his father while his brothers were in the army. David's father asked him to take lunch to his brothers at the camp."

Hearing about lunch, Boots shoved another kitty treat in her mouth.

Pooks continued, "David arrived and saw King Saul and his men of Israel fighting the Philistines. He went to go look for his brothers. When he found them, David's big brother told him of Goliath, the giant. David saw all the men of Israel were afraid. David asked, 'Who is this giant Goliath that is saying bad things about God's army?'"

Boots jumped on top of the park bench, acting like she was in battle. "David was not afraid at all, and I would not be either! I could have taken down Goliath too!"

Pooks shushed Boots before going on. "Yes, you are right, Boots, David was not afraid. He wanted to fight Goliath, but his brother did not want him to fight."

Michael and Kristy listened intently as Pooks continued, "When King Saul heard that David wanted to fight Goliath, he told David that he was too young."

Michael wrinkled his brow and looked down at his flyer, "Hey, that's what my teacher told me, that I was too young!"

Boots meowed with excitement, "That's right, that's right, now you're getting it!"

Pooks purred with contentment. "David told King Saul that he was a shepherd for his father's sheep, and he had protected his sheep from lions and bears! He was prepared for battle with all he had learned being a shepherd. He said, 'The Lord protected me from lions and bears, and He will protect me from Goliath.'"

Licking her paw Pooks turned the page, "King Saul saw how confident David was because of his faith in God, so he finally agreed and said, 'May the Lord be with you.' He gave David all of his own armor and weapons for battle."

"Here we go, here we go! We are going into battle!" Boots meowed loudly with excitement to hear the rest of the story.

Pooks's tail twitched as she watched Boots get excited. "David tried on the armor and said, 'I don't know how to use this armor. I will use what I know.' So David took the armor off, and picked up his shepherd staff. He grabbed five stones and put them in a bag. Then he grabbed his sling with his other hand and boldly went to face Goliath."

"I would have done the same thing," Boots said. "All I need are these paws of mine and God on my side!"

As everyone leaned in to hear what was going to happen next, Pooks's voice grew very serious. "Goliath saw David, and said, 'You are just a little boy!' Goliath went on and on as he made fun of David and called him names. Goliath said, 'You are going to fight me with a stick?'"

Pooks paused dramatically before she went on. "David was not worried or scared at all. He said to Goliath, 'You are going to fight me with a sword, spear and shield, but I come against you in the name of the Lord Almighty, the God of the armies of Israel, whom you have said bad things about! And I will defeat you because the Lord is on my side.'"

Boots started jumping up and down. "That is right, that is right, we got the Lord on our side!"

Pooks used both of her paws to show what happened next. "Goliath and David ran toward each other. David quickly put a stone in his sling, spun it around a few times, and slung it toward Goliath. The stone flew in the air with power and hit Goliath right in the middle of his forehead. Goliath fell down to the ground on his face!"

"Goliath is down, down for good!" Boots cheered with her paws victoriously in the air!

Michael and Kristy gave each other a high five as Pooks went on. "When the Philistines saw their champion Goliath had fallen and lost the battle, they ran away. Everyone was happy, and they all cheered for David! They all started dancing and celebrating, and King Saul made David a captain for his army!"

Everyone was jumping up and down with Boots, acting like they defeated Goliath!

"I got my answer, I got my answer!" Michael was still jumping up and down. "It is God! God is on my side, and I will win the competition. Everyone thought David was too young, just like they think I am too young! But that didn't matter, and it didn't stop him. David was prepared for the battle when he was a shepherd protecting his sheep from lions and bears. Just like David was prepared for battle, I was prepared for this competition when I won last year's science fair!"

Michael sat down, breathing hard again. "Thank you, Pooks! I knew you would give me the answer, it is God! I am confident God will be with me in this competition!"

Kristy admired Michael's confidence. "If David was the littlest and defeated the biggest giant, Goliath, then I can too! I can be the littlest on the basketball team and still win against the other team because God is with me!"

The next day, Michael rushed to get to school early. His mind was racing with ideas, but he still had to figure out the best solution. Going to the chalkboard, he started to write calculations furiously while drawing diagrams on how his rocket invention would work best.

Bruno was clueless of Michael's work. Chalk dust was flying in the air, and some of it landed on his nose. It tickled his nose and made him sneeze. He shook his head and looked back at all the drawings on the chalkboard. Bruno still didn't know what was going on but enjoyed listening to Michael mumble as he worked on his invention. He was glad to be a part of it anyway.

After some time, Michael stepped back and looked at his calculations one more time. He wiped a bit of chalk off his face and then gave Bruno a quick pat on the head. "We did it, Bruno! God is with us. This is going to work best. All I have to do now is convince my teacher." Michael was a little nervous after last time his teacher said he could not enter. However, he remembered how David wasn't nervous at all as he convinced King Saul to let him challenge the giant,

Goliath. Michael confidently knew he could convince his teacher to let him compete.

Michael and Bruno went down the hall to find his teacher. He found him sitting in his office grading papers. "I have the winning invention for the Space Academy Science Competition," Michael blurted as he ran into the office holding a bundle of notes with his calculations and diagrams.

His teacher looked up from his papers and took his glasses off. "Michael," he started, "I know you're excited, but as I told you before—"

Michael interrupted his teacher, "Yes, you think I'm too young, but I am prepared for this competition. I won last year's science fair, and now I have the winning idea for this year's competition. Let me show you how."

Michael laid out his notes in front of the teacher and told him how everything would work, clearly showing his teacher that his invention would improve spaceships for the astronauts. His teacher was quite impressed. When Michael finished explaining, his teacher sat back in his chair. "Michael, I think you have a good chance of winning the competition, but I have to warn you, the other students will be older and have more experience."

Michael gathered his notes. "It will be just like the story of David and Goliath. Do you know it?"

"I am very familiar with the story, yes," his teacher said with a faint smile. "May the Lord be with you."

While Michael had been working on his rocket invention, Kristy was busy practicing her basketball skills. Every day she saw her skills become better and better. Snowball watched her with confusion, not sure what was so important about throwing a ball into some hoop. Chasing birds would be so much more enjoyable. Snowball stretched out lazily in the sun and was glad Kristy was having fun anyway.

As the sun went down, Kristy put her basketball away and picked up Snowball to take her in for dinner. "Thanks for being with me, Snowball. I'm still a little worried about those bigger girls on the other team, but I am confident God will be with me."

Two weeks later, Pooks, Boots, and their friends got up early to go to the Space Academy Science Competition. Everyone wanted to see what Michael had invented for the spaceship.

Boots was chewing on her treats as she was looking at the inventions. She put her little paws on some of the projects with amazement.

Pooks grabbed her paws and said, "Don't touch the posters, Boots. We are just supposed to look, not touch!"

Pooks then gathered Michael and all their friends and prayed, "Dear Lord, thank you for being with Michael and helping him in this competition. Amen."

The judges looked all day at the inventions and finally went to the stage to announce the winner.

Everyone sat down eagerly to hear who won. Michael did not sit down. He smiled and started walking to the stage where the trophy was being presented. And Bruno was right by his side!

The older students were laughing at Michael because he was just a little boy thinking he won the competition.

However, Michael was confident, like David, that the God was with him. He knew he was going to win the competition.

By the time Michael got to the stage, the judges announced the winner.

"And the Space Academy Science Competition winner is…Michael!" Bruno wagged his tail high in the air, barking with excitement for Michael.

The older students stopped laughing and looked surprised.

Pooks and Boots flew across the air and onto the stage to congratulate Michael! Kristy and Snowball jumped up and down as the judge gave Michael the winning trophy!

39

Days passed as the final preparations were made to launch the rocket that would take Michael's invention to space. The night before the launch, Michael could hardly sleep.

The next morning, everyone gathered to see the rocket launch. They joined in with the final countdown. "Ten…nine…eight…seven…six…five…four… three…two…one…*blast off*." Pooks and Boots felt everything shake and rumble under their paws, as the mighty engines of the rocket roared and carried the rocket off the ground.

Kristy and Snowball were amazed at how high the rocket went into the sky! Michael smiled and touched Bruno's head, knowing God's plan for him came together.

Weeks later, Pooks, Boots, Michael, Bruno, and Snowball were excited to finally see Kristy play her first basketball game. They arrived early so they could have great seats at the bleachers.

Kristy had been practicing every day after school. She was a little nervous when she saw how big the other girls were but remembered that God was with her! She knew she could win the game even though she was the littlest, just like David won against the giant, Goliath.

With the sound of a horn, the game started! Pooks, Boots, Michael, Bruno, and Snowball were excited to see Kristy on the court, dribbling the ball around all the tall girls. Even though she was the littlest, nobody stopped her from getting the ball down the court! Snowball knew that God was with her!

Two seconds before the buzzer, Kristy charged down the court toward the basket, dribbling the ball. The whole crowd leapt to their feet with excitement! Kristy jumped into the air and made the final shot…it went *SWOOSH* right into the basket! The team won as the final buzzer sounded.

47

All the girls on her team picked her up and cheered her on! All of Kristy's friends came rushing on the court to join in the celebration.

The coach gave her a high five, "You did it! I knew you would be perfect for our team. I think we have a new captain for the team!"

Kristy gave her coach a huge smile, "All the glory goes to God! He was with me the whole time."

Pooks exchanged a knowing look with Boots as they nodded at each other. "I think Kristy and Michael learned the lesson about David and Goliath!"

"Amen!" Boots purred.

Everyone was still excited days later when Pooks, Boots, and all their friends were back in the park.

"That's right, that's right!" Boots squeaked excitedly. "Michael's going to build a giant rocket, so that Kristy can play basketball in space, and—"

Michael interrupted, "Well, basketball wouldn't work in space because there would be no gravity to dribble the ball, so…"

Pooks noticed one of them was not quite as excited as everyone else and went to check on him. "Is everything okay, Bruno?"

51

Bruno's ears perked up, "Michael and Kristy have done so much, and I want to do something special too. Michael was so good to adopt me, but I still have friends back in the shelter that need a home and someone to take care of them. I want to take care of them the same way David took care of his people. I want to give them a forever home, but I just don't know how."

Pooks thought for a moment and then had an idea. "Don't worry, Bruno, I know a friend that might be able to help. Trust in the Lord." Pooks turned back toward all their friends. "Hey, everyone, we need to go see someone, right now!"

Boots dropped half a kitty treat out of her mouth. "Mmph? Who are we going to see?"

Pooks purred, "An old friend of ours. Bandit!"

Pooks, Boots, Bruno, and their friends left the park and went across town. The houses kept getting bigger and bigger. Michael asked, "So, um…who is this Bandit guy we're going to see?"

Boots pounced around everyone as they kept walking. "Bandit is our oldest friend! We rescued him when we were lost in the wilderness, and we fixed his leg, and we played all sorts of games, and then this nice man took us to the shelter, and then we got adopted by Mommy and Daddy, and Bandit didn't at first, but then he got adopted by a family that had a royal cat named Prince Grey, and then…"

"Boots"—Pooks twitched her tail ever so slightly—"do you ever stop to breathe? Besides, it looks like we're here now."

Kristy looked at the house Pooks stopped at. It was the biggest house she had ever seen. "This house? Does Goliath live here? It's huge!"

Pooks went up to the door, and a deep chime rang in the distance. After a few moments, a man dressed in a black suit with white gloves and a very serious look on his face opened the door and quickly looked down to the small crowd on the porch. "Mistress Pooks, it has been far too long since you and Boots have come to visit. I see you have brought your friends. I presume you are here to see Master Bandit and Prince Grey?"

Pooks sat up straight as she used her most polite voice, "Yes, Mister Butler, you are correct. And it is a pleasure to see you again!"

Mister Butler could not stop a quiet chuckle. "Shall I prepare a blanket and some treats in the backyard for you all while you wait for Master Bandit and Prince Grey?"

Boots ran toward the backyard without waiting for Mister Butler to show them the way. "That's right, that's right! That would be great! You guys have the best kitty treats!"

"Boots! Behave yourself!" Pooks scolded, but it was too late. Boots was already out of sight.

Everyone was in the backyard and having fun, when Mister Butler emerged from the home carrying a purple pillow with a large fluffy gray cat wearing a crown. Behind them, a cat that was caramel-and-vanilla-and-chocolate-and-licorice all in one followed them with his tail high up in the air.

Seeing her friend, Boots dropped her kitty treat and ran toward the caramel-and-vanilla-and-chocolate-and-licorice cat. "BANDIT!" she howled in midair, as she tackled her friend and rumbled with him on the ground.

Bandit playfully pawed back at Boots. "It's good to see you too! I've missed you!"

Pooks nodded toward Mister Butler in thanks. "Everyone, this is Prince Grey. You probably figured out that is Bandit over there with Boots. Prince Grey, let me introduce you to our friends." Pooks then took some time and gave everyone a proper introduction to their old friends Bandit and Prince Grey.

Once introductions were complete, Mister Butler brought out trays full of kitty treats, kibbles, chicken chunks and gravy, bowls of water…and even a big juicy bone for Bruno. He even brought out cupcakes and lemonade for Kristy and Michael. Everyone was laughing and having a great time.

"I'm so glad you all came to visit," Prince Grey said. "But I'm sure there must be something on your mind."

"Indeed, there is," said Pooks. "Bruno here has a great idea about taking care of all the animals at the shelter that still need a forever home, but he needs some help. Bruno, would you care to tell Prince Grey all about your idea?"

Bruno gulped. "Um....I...um...I don't quite know what to say...All my friends at the shelter have been there so long, and I miss them and want to help take care of them the way David took care of his people, and I thought if I could just find a way to get a home for all of them..."

Bandit stopped wrestling with Boots when he heard Bruno talking about taking care of others. "You really are just like Pooks and Boots. They took good care of me when I was hurt, cold, and alone in the wilderness. You have a heart just like theirs."

"I remember you telling me about them," Prince Grey purred. "Many times. I would not have my best friend here if it was not for them. If Bruno has a heart like that, I would be honored to help him. We shall help build a beautiful forever home for all the animals."

"That's right, that's right!" Boots chimed in. "God was with us in the wilderness with Bandit, and He's with us now for all the animals!"

The following days and weeks were busy as the beautiful home for all the animals was built. Bruno went to the site every day to make sure everything with the home was made perfect and safe. Finally, the home was complete, and Prince Grey made sure the home was filled with plenty of food and lots of toys and soft beds for all the animals that would live there. It was almost ready to open.

"Wow…it sure looks good." Boots whistled as she walked through the shiny new home. She jumped on all the kitty condos and pounced on all the plush doggie beds. After trying everything out, she decided her favorite was the hammock! She looked around for a cardboard box but thought there were more than enough toys to make up for it.

"Yes, but it still needs one more thing…the most important detail." Prince Grey looked at Bruno. "You need to fill this house with lots of love to make it a home. Can you do that?"

Bruno wagged his tail vigorously. "I will! God helped David take care of his people, and He will help me take care of all the animals."

With that, Prince Grey smiled and turned to Mister Butler. "I think we are ready then. Bring everyone in!"

Mister Butler gave Prince Grey a slight bow then turned to the front door. He was nearly knocked down by all the animals rushing into their shiny new home. Everyone was laughing and having a good time. Mister Butler tried to say something to Prince Grey, but there was too much barking and meowing for anyone to hear. Boots and Bandit joined in, racing around to show their new friends the best places to nap in their new forever home.

Pooks hugged her Bible close to her, amazed by all the good things that had happened. She smiled as she thought about how much the story of David and Goliath helped them all. "God is with us. I think we should give a prayer of thanks." Everyone joined in prayer to thank God for the wonderful things He had done for them all.

Pooks, Boots, and friends continue to spend each day helping those in need. They pray you do the same.

Acknowledgments

I thank my Lord and Savior, Jesus Christ, for everything! He saved me, changed me, and continues to make me who I need to be. To God be the glory!

Michael J. Wood, my best friend and beloved husband, who held my hand every step of the way.

To my family, thank you for your loving support.

Simon Goodway, our wonderful illustrator who has been so patient working with me. Many people see our illustrations and think they are created in a snap, but the reality is far from that. Instead, one illustration can take weeks to create. Simon takes my detailed descriptions with an open heart—where to put Jesus in the picture, how I want my characters to appear, the colors, trees, the background—and blends them together, turning my vision into a reality.

To the entire publishing team that worked on my book at Covenant, especially Michelle Holmes. They did an exceptional job. They helped us get our books in the hands of children around the world.

William Robers, of Sparks Willson Borges Brandt and Johnson, has been an exceptional attorney for Pooks, Boots and Jesus LLC. He always ensures our company is protected and doing what we do best, serving the Lord.

To the shelters, orphanages, pastors, missionaries, ministries, and churches around the world that have used our books to teach children about Jesus, we are grateful.

To my precious kitties, Pooks and Boots, I thank them for their unconditional love. They inspire me to write about the love of Jesus every day. They are part of my heart, family, and this book series.

To everyone who has connected with us on our Pooks, Boots and Jesus Facebook page, your loving support has touched my heart. The stories, testimonies, and loving prayers for others have been such an inspiration. I am grateful for the wonderful connections that share the love of Jesus around the world.

About the Author

Julie K. Wood is the Author and Founder of Pooks, Boots and Jesus. The company is based on her book series and teaches the word of God in a new and fresh way.

Julie was a top award-winning officer in the United States Air Force. She has a Bachelor's degree in Clinical Laboratory Sciences and a Master of Arts in Education Curriculum and Instruction. She used her education and skills to become a successful flight commander, leading her team for eight and a half years. She loved serving her country and was selected to the rank of Major. She separated from the Air Force when she married her beloved husband, Michael J. Wood, who was an Air Force flight surgeon and now works at Kennedy Space Center for NASA as an Aerospace Medicine Physician for the astronauts.

Julie knows her background as an officer was not the final plan God had for her. She now serves the Lord full time with Pooks, Boots and Jesus.

She would love to see you connect with Pooks, Boots and Jesus on their Facebook page at www.facebook.com/pooksbootsandjesus.

You can also visit their website at www.pooksbootsandjesus.com.

For more information on Julie, you can find her Amazon author page at https://www.amazon.com/author/juliekwood.

Stay tuned! Julie is working with Pooks and Boots on their next adventure!

CPSIA information can be obtained
at www.ICGtesting.com
Printed in the USA
BVHW022306010322
630318BV00011B/718